Samuel French Acting Edit

M000188076

The Legend of Sleepy Hollow

Written by
John Heimbuch

Created in collaboration with
Jon Ferguson

Based on the story by
Washington Irving

FOR PRODUCTION INQUIRIES

UNITED STATES AND CANADA
info@concordtheatricals.com
1-866-979-0447

UNITED KINGDOM AND EUROPE
licensing@concordtheatricals.co.uk
020-7054-7200

Each title is subject to availability from Concord Theatricals Corp., depending upon country of performance. Please be aware that *THE LEGEND OF SLEEPY HOLLOW* may not be licensed by Concord Theatricals Corp. in your territory. Professional and amateur producers should contact the nearest Concord Theatricals Corp. office or licensing partner to verify availability.

MUSIC AND THIRD PARTY MATERIALS USE NOTE

Licensees are solely responsible for obtaining formal written permission from copyright owners to use copyrighted music and/or other copyrighted third-party materials (e.g., artworks, logos) in the performance of this play and are strongly cautioned to do so. If no such permission is obtained by the licensee, then the licensee must use only original music and materials that the licensee owns and controls. Licensees are solely responsible and liable for clearances of all third-party copyrighted materials, including without limitation music, and shall indemnify the copyright owners of the play(s) and their licensing agent, Concord Theatricals Corp., against any costs, expenses, losses and liabilities arising from the use of such copyrighted third-party materials by licensees. For music, please contact the appropriate music licensing authority in your territory for the rights to any incidental music.

IMPORTANT BILLING AND CREDIT REQUIREMENTS

If you have obtained performance rights to this title, please refer to your licensing agreement for important billing and credit requirements.

THE LEGEND OF SLEEPY HOLLOW originally premiered on October 30, 2010 at the Rural America Arts Center in Plainview, Minnesota for a run of nineteen performances. It was directed by Jon Ferguson and produced by the Jon Hassler Theater, and staged with the following cast:

ICHABOD CRANE . . . . Ryan Lear

KATRINA VAN TASSEL . . . . Joanna Harmon

BROM BONES. . . . . Brant Miller

GEOFFREY CRAYON, PARSON VAN HOUTEN,
    RUPERT, ETC.. . . . . Tony Sarnicki

BALTUS VAN TASSEL, COUNTRY GIRL, ETC.. . . . . Sara Richardson

HANS VAN RIPPER, GUNPOWDER,
    SKELETON, ETC.. . . . . Kimberly Richardson

OLD MAN 1, COUNTRY GIRL, STUDENT, ETC.. . . . . Meghan Hernick

OLD MAN 2, COUNTRY GIRL, STUDENT, ETC.. . . . . . Piper Lin Sigel-Bruse

OLD MAN 3, COUNTRY GIRL, STUDENT, ETC.. . . . . .Ashton Schneider

HORSEMAN, OTTO VAN LANCKER, STUDENT, ETC.. . . . . Hans Hauge

The production team included sets by Erica Zaffarano, sound and music by Tim Cameron, costumes by Lori Opsal, lights by Kathy Maxwell, choreography by Kimberly Richardson, puppets by Joanna Harmon, and stage management by Jenna Johnson.

THE LEGEND OF SLEEPY HOLLOW was subsequently produced on February 9, 2013 at the Red Eye Theater in Minneapolis, Minnesota for a run of fifteen performances. It was directed by Jon Ferguson and produced by Walking Shadow Theatre Company, and staged with the following cast:

ICHABOD CRANE . . . . Ryan Lear

KATRINA VAN TASSEL . . . . Joanna Harmon

BROM BONES. . . . . Brant Miller

GEOFFREY CRAYON, PARSON VAN HOUTEN,
    RUPERT, ETC.. . . . . Casey Hoekstra

BALTUS VAN TASSEL, COUNTRY GIRL, ETC.. . . . . Susanna Stahlmann

HANS VAN RIPPER, GUNPOWDER, SKELETON, ETC.. . . . . . . Suzy Kohane

OLD MAN 1, COUNTRY GIRL, STUDENT, ETC. . . . . Kenzi Allen

OLD MAN 2, COUNTRY GIRL, STUDENT, ETC. . . . . . Piper Lin Sigel-Bruse

OLD MAN 3, COUNTRY GIRL, STUDENT, ETC. . . . . .Ashton Schneider

HORSEMAN, OTTO VAN LANCKER, STUDENT, ETC. . . . . Hans Hauge

The production team included sets by Erica Zaffarano, sound and music by Tim Cameron, costumes by Lori Opsal, lights by Logan Jambik, puppets by Joanna Harmon, dialect coaching by Keely Wolter, and stage management by Callie Meiners.

CHARACTERS

ICHABOD CRANE – a Connecticut schoolteacher

GEOFFREY CRAYON – a New Yorker of distinction

BROM BONES – a roistering blade

KATRINA VAN TASSEL – a country coquette

BALTUS VAN TASSEL – a gentleman farmer

HANS VAN RIPPER – another gentleman farmer

PARSON VAN HOUTEN – a man of faith

RUPERT VAN BRUNT – a spiteful schoolboy

GUNPOWDER – a weatherbeaten nag

OTTO VAN LANCKER – a willing believer

OLD BROUWER – a willful disbeliever

HEADLESS HORSEMAN – a headless Hessian mercenary

VILLAGERS

STUDENTS

COUNTRY GIRLS

SLEEPY HOLLOW BOYS

OLD MEN

A SKELETON

The play may be performed by a cast of ten. The roles of Ichabod and Brom Bones should be played by performers who identify as male. The role of Katrina should be played by a performer who identifies as female. These three roles should not double. All other roles may be played by anyone in the ensemble.

SETTING

On the continent of North America,
in the country of The United States,
in the state of New York,
in the region of Tarrytown
is the village of Sleepy Hollow.

TIME

Autumn, 1801.

AUTHOR'S NOTES

The original productions included many improvisations and embellishments from the ensemble, which have been omitted from this script. You are welcome to devise your own within the context of the play.

The ensemble is responsible for creating the environment and atmosphere of the play. Scenic transitions should be achieved through the simplicity of the staging and the playfulness of the ensemble.

A heightened melodramatic style would be very appropriate.

Dutch accents for the villagers will add to the fun.

The Legend of Sleepy Hollow *was originally commissioned by the Jon Hassler Theater in 2010, and further developed by Walking Shadow Theatre Company in 2013.*

For Dean and Sally.

(A long-vacant room. Leaves litter the floor. A table brims over with handwritten papers. There is a portrait of **ICHABOD CRANE** *on the wall – looking haughty.)*

(Rattling keys. A door creaks open. Light spills in.)

*(***GEOFFREY CRAYON*** enters, a New York gentleman of 1817 – modern in every way. He looks around the room, and makes his way to the table.)*

(He discovers a page.)

GEOFFREY. *(Reading.)* "If I can but reach that bridge," thought Ichabod, "I am safe."

> *(He puts it down. He picks up another.)*

The papers of the late Diedrich Knickerbocker.

> *(The portrait of* **ICHABOD** *smiles. Did he just see that?)*
>
> *(***GEOFFREY*** digs through the pages until he finds what he believes to be the beginning. He starts reading. The words are strange at first, but with growing familiarity.)*

In the bosom of one of those spacious coves which indent the eastern shore of the Hudson, at that broad expansion of the river denominated by the ancient Dutch navigators the Tappan Zee, there lies a small market-town, which is generally and properly known by the name of Tarrytown. Not far from this village, there is a little valley among high hills, which is one of the quietest places in the whole world. A small brook glides through it, with just murmur enough to lull one to a slumber.

> *(He flips pages.)*

From the listless repose of the place, and the peculiar character of its inhabitants, who are descendants from the original Dutch settlers, this sequestered glen has long been known by the name of SLEEPY HOLLOW.

> (**VILLAGERS** *emerge. They gather up logs and branches.*)

A drowsy, dreamy influence seems to hang over the land. Some say that the place was bewitched by a high German doctor; others, that an old Indian chief held his pow-wows there before the country was discovered by Master Hendrick Hudson. Certain it is, the place still continues under the sway of some witching power, that holds a spell over the minds of the good people, causing them to walk in a continual reverie. The whole neighborhood abounds with local tales, haunted spots, and twilight superstitions; stars shoot and meteors glare oftener across the valley than in any other part of the country. The dominant spirit that haunts this enchanted region is the apparition of a figure on horseback –

> (*The* **VILLAGERS** *use the branches and logs to enact the* **HEADLESS HORSEMAN** *riding through the woods.*)

– without a head.

> (**ICHABOD**'s *portrait becomes terrified!*)

It is said by some to be the ghost of a Hessian trooper, whose head had been carried away by a cannonball, in some nameless battle during the Revolutionary War; having been buried in the churchyard, he rides forth to the scene of battle in nightly quest of his head; and that rushing speed with which he sometimes passes along the Hollow, like a midnight blast, is owing to his hurry to get back to the churchyard before daybreak. And the specter is known, at all the country firesides, by the name of THE HEADLESS HORSEMAN OF SLEEPY HOLLOW!

> (*The rush of hooves.*)

(The furniture is whisked away. Everyone disappears.)

*(Two **VILLAGERS** enter theatrically.)*

VILLAGER 1. In Sleepy Hollow, as in all such little retired Dutch valleys embosomed in the great State of New York, the population, manners, and customs of old remained fixed and constant.

*(**PARSON VAN HOUTEN** and **HANS VAN RIPPER** enter theatrically.)*

VILLAGER 2. Indeed, it would be no great surprise to find the same families vegetating in its sheltered bosom as when its farms were first settled, still bearing such proud family names as:

*(**BALTUS VAN TASSEL** and **BROM BONES** enter theatrically.)*

PARSON VAN HOUTEN. Van Houten.

HANS VAN RIPPER. Van Ripper.

BALTUS VAN TASSEL. Van Tassel.

BROM BONES. Or Van Brunt.

*(Another **VILLAGER** enters theatrically.)*

VILLAGER 3. Nor was the fearful propensity of its citizens confined to the native inhabitants of the valley, but it is unconsciously imbibed by everyone who resides there for a time.

*(A final **VILLAGER** enters theatrically.)*

VILLAGER 4. However wide awake they may have been before they entered that sleepy region, they are sure to soon inhale the witching influence of the air, grow imaginative and see apparitions.

(Everyone listens. Footsteps in the distance. Whistling.)

VILLAGER 1. It was in this noted byplace of nature that there abode a worthy wight by the name:

*(**ICHABOD** emerges – confident, eager, lanky.)*

ICHABOD. Ichabod Crane.

> *(He gestures with dramatic flourish.)*

> *(The **VILLAGERS** eye him suspiciously.)*

Yes. Hello. Um. I'm the new schoolteacher. From Connecticut. Yale, actually.

VILLAGERS 1 & 3. An exceedingly lank fellow!

ICHABOD. They said I was a scholar of the first order. Well versed in religion, science, and language.

VILLAGERS 2 & 5. His hands dangle a mile out of his sleeves!

ICHABOD. One of a legion of country schoolteachers unleashed to teach the children of these towns.

BROM. Head like a weathervane!

ICHABOD. But I'm eager to make a happy home here in Sleepy Hollow.

VILLAGERS. Ah.

> *(The **VILLAGERS** go about their business.)*

ICHABOD. Hello. A pleasure to make your – uh.

> *(**KATRINA VAN TASSEL** appears at a distance – a peculiar and beautiful young villager.)*

> *(**ICHABOD** sees her. Instantly smitten.)*

Oh!

> *(**ICHABOD** rushes through the **VILLAGERS** to reach her.)*

Excuse me. Pardon me. Excuse me.

> *(**KATRINA** and **BROM** share a look.)*

> *(**ICHABOD** and **KATRINA** share a look.)*

> *(**ICHABOD** and **BROM** share a look.)*

> *(**KATRINA** and **BROM** exit in opposite directions.)*

> *(The **VILLAGERS** enact the descriptions of **ICHABOD**.)*

VILLAGER 5. To see him striding along the profile of a hill on a windy day, with his clothes bagging and fluttering about him anyone could mistake him for the spirit of famine descending upon the earth.

VILLAGER 4. Or a scarecrow eloped from a cornfield.

> (**ICHABOD** *claps his hands. A schoolroom assembles.*)
>
> (*The* **VILLAGERS** *become attentive* **STUDENTS**.)
>
> (**RUPERT VAN BRUNT** *stands in the corner, dunce cap on his head.*)

ICHABOD. In matters of education I shall be most attentive to the minds of my students, taking great care to instruct them in matters sure to be of use in their lives.

> (*To the* **STUDENTS**.)

According to Cotton Mather's treatise on the peril of witchcraft in New England, we are at all times beset by the devil and his minions. Ghosts and demons of the netherworld ever seek to impart their mischief upon us, and if one does not exercise suitable caution they may turn their attentions to you.

STUDENT 1. Aaah!

ICHABOD. Or you.

STUDENT 2. Aaah!

ICHABOD. Or you!

STUDENT 3. Aaah!

ICHABOD. And whisk you off to hell at once!

STUDENTS. Aaaah!

> (**ICHABOD** *silences them. He turns away.*)

ICHABOD. Now who can tell me what must be done with the devil at your back?

> (*The* **STUDENTS** *look at each other, mischievous.*)
>
> (*He turns around. The* **STUDENTS** *prank* **ICHABOD**.)
>
> (*He falls back in fear.*)

Aaaaah!

> (*The* **STUDENTS** *laugh uproariously.*)

(ICHABOD stands.)

ICHABOD. *(Cont.)* Quiet! Quiet I say!!

> *(The STUDENTS are immediately silent.)*
>
> *(Except RUPERT, who just laughs louder.)*

Rupert. Rupert. Rupert Van Brunt. Come here!

> **(RUPERT** *stops. Filled with dread. He steps forward.)*

Well, young scholar, your parents have paid me to provide your education, and so I must do my duty by them to see that you get it. But I assure you, you will remember this and thank me for it on the longest day you live.

> **(ICHABOD** *pushes* **RUPERT** *to his knees.)*
>
> **(ICHABOD** *holds out his hand.)*
>
> *(Another* **STUDENT** *hands him a birch branch.)*

Children, we call this the Golden Maxim:

RUPERT. The Golden Maxim!

ICHABOD. Spare the rod and spoil the child. And I'll have you know, young sir, that Ichabod Crane's scholars are certainly not spoiled.

> **(ICHABOD** *uses the switch on* **RUPERT.** *Three sharp strikes.)*

Corner.

> **(ICHABOD** *pinches* **RUPERT**'*s ear and deposits him back in the corner.)*
>
> **(RUPERT** *rubs his backside.* **ICHABOD** *strikes his hand.)*
>
> **(RUPERT** *starts to cry.)*
>
> **(ICHABOD** *hands the switch back to the* **STUDENT.)***

Now, who would like to read the next section?

> *(All the* **STUDENTS** *raise their hands.)*

(ICHABOD *points at* STUDENT 2 *and exits.*)

(STUDENT 2 *stands. The other* STUDENTS *scatter.*)

STUDENT 2. But Ichabod Crane was no grim authoritarian. Indeed, on holiday afternoons, he would even convoy some of the smaller boys home. Especially those who happened to have pretty sisters, or plentiful farms, or doting mothers noted for the comforts of the cupboard.

(RUPERT *runs off, shouting:*)

RUPERT. Brom! Brom!

STUDENT 2. Given the peculiar character of the inhabitants, it should be no surprise that there were some who were known to play tricks upon the frightened minds of the townsfolk.

(STUDENT 2 *is whisked away.*)

(KATRINA *enters with several* COUNTRY GIRLS.)

(*They look around.*)

COUNTRY GIRLS. He's not here yet.

KATRINA. No, he's not.

(*The* SLEEPY HOLLOW BOYS *swagger in. A rowdy bunch of country hooligans.*)

COUNTRY GIRLS. These charming rowdy fellows were known as the Sleepy Hollow Boys.

SLEEPY HOLLOW BOYS. Ja!

(BROM BONES *enters. Proud and powerful.*)

COUNTRY GIRL 1. The most formidable of which was a burly, roaring, roistering blade, of the name:

BROM. Abraham Van Brunt!

COUNTRY GIRL 2. Known to his friends as:

SLEEPY HOLLOW BOYS. Brom Bones!

(BROM *does a secret handshake with the other* SLEEPY HOLLOW BOYS.)

COUNTRY GIRL 1. He was foremost at all races and cock-fights.

COUNTRY GIRL 2. And well renowned throughout the valley for his superior strength, horsemanship, and hardiness.

> *(One of the **SLEEPY HOLLOW BOYS** challenges Brom to a leg-wrestling contest.)*

SLEEPY HOLLOW BOYS: Brom Brom Brom!

> *(**BROM** defeats his challenger easily.)*

> *(**BROM** helps him up and embraces him.)*

BROM. Brother.

COUNTRY GIRLS. Braaa-m.

> *(**BROM** points at them. Boom. The **COUNTRY GIRLS** faint, leaving **KATRINA** standing alone.)*

BROM. But even the mighty Brom Bones had one challenge he couldn't overcome.

KATRINA. Brom.

BROM. Katrina.

KATRINA. Enjoying yourself?

BROM. Well enough.

KATRINA. Still playing with the boys?

SLEEPY HOLLOW BOYS. Ja.

BROM. No.

> *(**BROM** dismisses the **SLEEPY HOLLOW BOYS**. They exit.)*

We only live so long. Better enjoy it while we can.

KATRINA. Hmm.

BROM. What?

KATRINA. Nothing.

BROM. Right. Uh, say, Katrina – I was wondering…

KATRINA. Be careful what you ask, Brom.

BROM. All right.

> *(**BROM** takes her hand and goes to one knee. Mockingly.)*

I wonder if a pretty young girl like you – and a rough, uncouth, unmannered country swain like me –

(KATRINA pulls her hand away.)

KATRINA. Let me know when you're ready to grow up.

(She exits.)

(BROM shouts in frustration.)

(RUPERT enters, now carrying the dunce cap.)

RUPERT. Brom?

BROM BONES. What!?

(He softens.)

What? Rupert, what is it?

(RUPERT whispers in BROM's ear.)

(RUPERT gestures three times. Thwack! Thwack! Thwack!)

(BROM's eyes narrow.)

I see.

(BROM puts an arm around RUPERT. They exit.)

(A gnarled old man appears. This is HANS VAN RIPPER.)

HANS. According to country custom the schoolmaster would board and lodge at the houses of the farmers whose children he instructed. Going the rounds of the neighborhood each week with all his worldly effects tied up in a cotton handkerchief.

(ICHABOD knocks on the door.)

(HANS opens the door.)

(ICHABOD enters with his bindle. He looks around.)

ICHABOD. Hans Van Reaper?

HANS. It's Van Ripper! Well, you might as well come in, since you're in.

(Hoofbeats race by in the distance.)

ICHABOD. Goodness. What's that?

HANS. Ay, there goes Brom Bones and his gang!

> *(**HANS** closes the door.)*

> *(**BALTUS VAN TASSEL** opens the door theatrically – the village's most prosperous citizen.)*

BALTUS. Hans.

HANS. Baltus.

> *(They bow to each other in the old style.)*

BALTUS. Is this him?

HANS. Yep.

BALTUS. Mynheer Crane. Welcome to Sleepy Hollow. I am Baltus Van Tassel.

ICHABOD. Yes sir, hello. And a pleasure it is to be here!

BALTUS. Yes. You have been hired by the town council to educate our children, is that not so?

ICHABOD. Oh yes. I am well versed in arithmetic, geometry, Latin, swimming –

BALTUS. Singing?

ICHABOD. Swimming.

BALTUS. Singing!

ICHABOD. What?

BALTUS. We hear your infernal whistling all through the valley. I can only imagine you must know a song or two.

ICHABOD. Oh, yes. Thank you.

BALTUS. I suppose you could instruct my daughter Katrina on the finer points of the art? Katrina! Katrina! Katrina…

> *(**KATRINA** appears in the doorway.)*

> *(**ICHABOD** sees her and gasps.)*

She is young and eager to learn. Isn't that true?

KATRINA. Yes.

BALTUS. Better than spending all of her time with that incorrigible Van Brunt boy. But as Parson Van Houten is too busy to instruct her, you will have to do. The pay won't be much, but I will see that you're well provided for come harvest time. Will you undertake this?

ICHABOD. Oh. Yes. Gladly.

BALTUS. Katrina, Mynheer Crane has agreed to be your singing teacher.

KATRINA. I heard.

BALTUS. How soon can you begin?

ICHABOD. Oh, immediately. If you wish.

BALTUS. You've finished all your other work for the day?

ICHABOD. Oh, I expect I can find the time in my schedule.

BALTUS. Then I hope you will join us at our farm this evening.

ICHABOD. Of course. Is it very far from here?

BALTUS. A few miles down the road, near Major Andre's Tree.

ICHABOD. Major Andre's Tree?

BALTUS. You don't know it?

*(They all turn to look at **ICHABOD**.)*

ICHABOD. No…

BALTUS. A great tulip tree that towers over the rest of the wood, and which has grown twisted and gnarled on account of its age.

*(**HANS** gnarls and twists.)*

Running along its eastern side is a streak of white where it was scarred by a thunderbolt!

HANS. Kabooom.

BALTUS. It was under this tree where the fateful Major Andre was caught transporting secrets for the British during the war. And after his execution, it's said that the tree creaked and groaned as though under great duress.

*(**HANS** creaks and groans.)*

BALTUS. *(Cont.)* And ever since there have been all manner of troublesome sightings in its vicinity – phantom funeral processions, unearthly music, and vile apparitions! It's even said that John Andre's hanged body is sometimes seen dangling from its branches – which any old wife knows is a sure sign that the viewer will die within ten days time.

KATRINA. Oooooo.

ICHABOD. And you live near this tree?

BALTUS. Oh, yes. Very close. I'll expect you there just after sunset.

ICHABOD. I'm not entirely sure that I should –

BALTUS. There will be all manner of cakes and pies.

ICHABOD. I shall be there.

BALTUS. Don't be late. Her education is in your hands.

ICHABOD. I will do my best!

KATRINA. See you tonight, Mynheer Crane.

BALTUS. Good day Hans!

HANS. Meh!

> (**BALTUS** *and* **HANS** *bow in the old style again.*)
>
> (**BALTUS** *and* **KATRINA** *exit.*)

ICHABOD. …Katrina Van Tassel…

HANS. Eh?

ICHABOD. What?

HANS. Nothing. Let's get you settled.

ICHABOD. Yes, thank you. And if you need any help around the farm, my hands will make light work of your tasks.

> (**HANS** *looks at* **ICHABOD**'s *smooth hands.*)

HANS. Ja. Right! No thanks!

> (**HANS** *takes* **ICHABOD**'s *bindle and exits.*)
>
> (*Several* **COUNTRY GIRLS** *enter and surround* **ICHABOD**.)

COUNTRY GIRL 1. The schoolmaster is generally considered a man of some importance in the female circle of a rural neighborhood.

ICHABOD. A touch of culture in the rustic setting, a kind of gentlemanlike personage, of vastly superior taste and accomplishments to the rough country swains, and, indeed, inferior in learning only to the parson.

(More **COUNTRY GIRLS** *surround* **ICHABOD***.)*

COUNTRY GIRL 2. Ichabod Crane was known to pass at least a few of his idle hours in the smiles of the country damsels.

COUNTRY GIRL 3. Reciting for their amusement all the epitaphs on the tombstones:

ICHABOD. "In Lives Full Joys And Virtuous Fare of Bloom
Untimely Check and Hurried To The Tomb
Life How Short, Eternity How Long."

COUNTRY GIRL 1. Or sauntering, with a whole bevy of them, along the banks of the adjacent mill-pond.

*(***ICHABOD*** *and the* **COUNTRY GIRLS** *saunter.)*

ICHABOD. Oh look, a bird.

COUNTRY GIRLS. Ooo.

*(***BROM*** *enters. He lurks at a distance.)*

ICHABOD. While the more bashful country bumpkins hung sheepishly back, envying my superior elegance and address.

(The **COUNTRY GIRLS** *laugh.)*

BROM. Ichabod Crane!

*(***BROM*** *points at the* **COUNTRY GIRLS***. Boom!)*

(They faint, leaving **ICHABOD** *at the center.)*

ICHABOD. Yes? Hello?

BROM. You're the new schoolmaster.

ICHABOD. That's right.

BROM. I'm told you're renowned throughout the valley for leaving a mark of knowledge on your students.

ICHABOD. Thank you, yes. I certainly try.

BROM. So I hear. I thought I'd like to see you with my own eyes. Determine what sort of mettle makes this man.

ICHABOD. Yes, well, here I am, in the flesh.

BROM. What there is of it.

> (*The* **COUNTRY GIRLS** *giggle.*)
>
> (**BROM** *silences them with a gesture.*)
>
> (*The* **COUNTRY GIRLS** *scatter.*)

ICHABOD. Sorry, do I know you?

BROM. No. Abraham Van Brunt.

> (**BROM** *raises his hand.* **ICHABOD** *steps back.*)
>
> (*A handshake.* **BROM** *has a very strong grip.*)

ICHABOD. Ah. And what do you do, Mr. Van Brunt?

BROM. I've been known to do any number of things in my time.

ICHABOD. So you're a renaissance man!

BROM. Is that what they call it?

ICHABOD. Yes.

BROM. Then I'm one of those.

ICHABOD. How reassuring to know there are some other enlightened fellows in this little burg. I have begun to feel quite like an island in this valley. The character of the inhabitants is quite resistant to knowledge, and just between you and me, too many of these country folk are content to never let their minds wander beyond the confines of their farms. My work is all the more difficult for it.

BROM. What work?

ICHABOD. Shining the beacon of knowledge into the darkest recesses of the mind. It is a perilous task, of course, apt to be misconstrued by the ignorant as pompous, high-minded rhetoric. I'm even told that schoolmasters have sometimes been known to suffer the most mischievous pranks by the bullies of their town who, for whatever reason, object to the pure edification of the soul.

BROM. Imagine that.

ICHABOD. But I am determined not to let such waggish behavior thwart me.

BROM. Do you plan to remain in Sleepy Hollow?

ICHABOD. Yes. Though my rustic patrons are apt to consider the costs of schooling a grievous burden, by hook and by crook, I shall make a name for myself here. I've already been hired as a singing instructor to supplement my daily bread, and am determined to find yet more ways of rendering myself both useful and agreeable to my miserly hosts who understand nothing of the labor of headwork. I'm sure it's only a matter of time before I find some marriageable young woman with a well-appointed farm and settle down properly.

BROM. Any prospects?

(They pause while **KATRINA** *crosses upstage.)*

ICHABOD. One, perhaps. But it's far too soon to say. Are you married, Mr. Van Brunt?

(They pause while **KATRINA** *crosses back.)*

KATRINA. Oh, I forgot something.

(And she's gone.)

BROM. Not yet, but maybe soon, God willing.

ICHABOD. Well, I wish us both the best of luck, though I very much doubt we'll need it. The rest of these Sleepy Hollow folk can scarcely compete with men of our character.

BROM. As you say. I'm glad to have met you, Mynheer Crane.

ICHABOD. You as well, Mr. Van Brunt.

BROM. And don't worry about any of those meddlesome country ruffians. I'll be more than happy to keep my eye on you.

ICHABOD. Thank you, sir. Always good to have another friendly face.

BROM. Good. I hoped you would think so.

>   (**BROM** *laughs. A little too long.*)

>   (**ICHABOD** *starts to laugh with him.*)

No! Only me!

>   (**BROM** *laughs even harder.*)

>   (**BROM** *races out.*)

Daredevil! Away! Hyah!

>   (*Hoofbeats.*)

>   (*And with a whoosh of wind,* **BROM** *is gone.*)

>   (**KATRINA** *appears in the picture frame.*)

KATRINA. That evening, as Ichabod walked down the long country road, he barely noticed the cold twinge in the air or the crisp crunch of leaves underfoot. Instead his mind raced with thoughts of the beautiful Katrina –

KATRINA & ICHABOD. A blooming lass of fresh eighteen, cute as a partridge, ripe and melting and rosy cheeked as one of her father's peaches.

ICHABOD. Yet she is a bit of a coquette, as might be perceived in her dress, though it certainly sets off her charms. And a provokingly short petticoat, to display the prettiest foot and ankle in the country round! But how to turn her affections toward me?

>   (**ICHABOD** *approaches the picture frame.*)

>   (**KATRINA** *pushes him away.*)

Oh these country girls! These country girls!

KATRINA. But as the sun set in the west, Ichabod's thoughts slowly turned away from such delightfiul possibilities, until he reached the towering Major Andre's Tree.

>   (**ICHABOD** *stands in awe of the tree.*)

And seeing no ghost in its lanky branches…

ICHABOD. Whew!

KATRINA. ...he turned down the path to the Van Tassel family farm. And oh, there on that path what did he smell?

(**ICHABOD** *smells something wonderful.*)

ICHABOD. Apple pies, sweet cakes, smoked ham, roast goose.

KATRINA. As he approached, he saw that the stable was filled with horses – including a dark one far more spirited than the rest.

(*Whinny of a horse.*)

And the farm itself was a-bustle with friends and family.

(**VILLAGERS** *prepare the house.*)

For to judge by the warmth of the home and the lay of the food, Baltus Van Tassel was a most generous host.

(**BALTUS** *unveils a table of cakes.*)

BALTUS. Mynheer Crane!

(**BALTUS** *opens the door.* **ICHABOD** *enters the house.*)

Katrina will be along shortly.

ICHABOD. Ah. I see you have any number of cakes.

BALTUS. Yes, there are five of them. Though I'll understand if you wish to keep the voice clear for the lesson.

ICHABOD. No matter, no matter.

(**ICHABOD** *reaches for a cake...*)

(*But* **PARSON VAN HOUTEN** *emerges and takes his hand.*)

PARSON VAN HOUTEN. Mynheer Van Tassel, is this the new schoolteacher?

ICHABOD. I am sir.

BALTUS. This is Parson Van Houten.

ICHABOD. Ah, Parson, I owe you my thanks.

PARSON VAN HOUTEN. For what?

ICHABOD. Bringing me here as the schoolmaster, of course.

PARSON VAN HOUTEN. I've done you no favors. And you owe me no thanks but your duty. Your task is nothing short of God's work. Mynheer Crane, as schoolteacher for this valley it is expected that you will be a role model for the parish youth – illustrating by example the value of literacy, sobriety, honesty, and civility. Now, I know you are from Connecticut.

(Laughter.)

So I hope you will appreciate what dangers such worldliness can spark in our students. I'm sure you have already found that our parishioners are no strangers to cussing, pranking, tall tales, and all manner of devilry in their lives. You must stand tall against such things, and show them that though myths and ghostly suppositions may run rampant within their minds, as a matter of course, such things will gain no traction against upstanding members of the church. For the faithful should have no cause to fear the devil's tricks. Right?

ICHABOD. What?

PARSON VAN HOUTEN. You are a believer?

ICHABOD. Oh. Yes.

PARSON VAN HOUTEN. Many of our former schoolteachers have seen the position as one of idle repose, enjoying the comforts of the cupboard and acting as some sort of town gossip, sharing whatever tidbits they acquired around the hearth, using their position for their own betterment rather than the betterment of the students. Is it then any wonder why they no longer hold this post?

ICHABOD. No. Of course.

PARSON VAN HOUTEN. I trust you will do your duty with patience and diligence. Now, if you'll excuse me, the road is long, and I have a sermon to prepare. Good day Mynheer Van Tassel. I shall see you at church tomorrow morning.

*(*BALTUS *escorts* PARSON VAN HOUTEN *out.)*

(**ICHABOD** *grabs a small cake.*)

(**KATRINA** *enters.* **BROM** *follows her.*)

(**ICHABOD** *eats his cake, oblivious.*)

BROM. Katrina, please, listen to me.

KATRINA. Not until you ask. Why will you not ask?

BROM. Because, Katrina… I have very strong…feelings… but…

KATRINA. Brom, you are hopeless. If you will not ask, what am I to do? I cannot wait forever! Or shall I wither on the vine while you decide what to do?

BROM. No.

KATRINA. I've a good mind to turn my attentions elsewhere. How would you like that?

(**KATRINA** *looks pointedly at* **ICHABOD**.)

BROM. I wouldn't like it.

KATRINA. No you wouldn't, would you? Not that you'd get any say in it. And even if you tried I'm sure my new friend will be quick to defend my honor.

ICHABOD. *(Eating, unaware.)* What?

BROM. What new friend? Is there someone else?

ICHABOD. *(Eating, unaware.)* What? Mmm.

KATRINA. I don't know. Maybe. Perhaps there is.

BROM. Who?

KATRINA. No one you'd know. Someone quite unlike any of the other men of the valley.

(**BROM** *finally gets it.*)

ICHABOD. *(Eating, unaware.)* This is the best traditional small cake I've ever had.

BROM. You aren't serious.

KATRINA. What if I am?

BROM. Then I will do something very bad to him.

KATRINA. And hurt the one I love?

BROM. How can you do this to me?

KATRINA. I'm sorry Brom, it's not my fault. You brought it on yourself. Mynheer Crane?

> (**ICHABOD** *turns, his mouth full of cake.*)

I am ready for my singing lesson now.

> (**ICHABOD** *swallows the cake.*)

ICHABOD. Mmm yes, Miss Van Tassel, nothing would give me greater pleasure.

> (**BROM** *gasps. He turns to go, and stumbles.*)
>
> (*Anger and embarrassment fill his face.*)
>
> (*As he is about to leave,* **ICHABOD** *finally notices him.*)

Ah, Mr. Van Brunt.

BROM. WHAT?

ICHABOD. So good to see you!

BROM. Goodbye Katrina.

KATRINA. Goodbye Brom.

> (**BROM** *clutches his hat and leaves. Slam.*)

BROM. DAREDEVIL! HYAH!

> (*Hoofbeats.*)
>
> (*And with a whoosh of wind,* **BROM** *is gone.*)
>
> (**KATRINA** *turns to* **ICHABOD**.)

KATRINA. Well?

ICHABOD. Well, what?

KATRINA. Are you going to teach me singing?

ICHABOD. Ah yes, well – it all starts with the voice.

> (**ICHABOD** *sings a single note. Nasal. Long.*)

Go ahead.

> (**KATRINA** *sings a single note. Ouch.*)

Very good, Miss Katrina. Now, I wonder if I might ask –

> (**ICHABOD** *takes her hand and bends to one knee.*)
>
> (*But* **BALTUS** *stands him back up.*)

BALTUS. Many thanks for your lesson, Mynheer Crane. But now I fear you must go.

ICHABOD. Go? But I was about to ask a question.

BALTUS. I fear it shall have to wait. For you must journey home at once. And do beware as you do!

ICHABOD. Beware?

KATRINA. Father –

ICHABOD. Beware of what?

KATRINA. The Horseman.

ICHABOD. The Horseman?

BALTUS. The Hessian Horseman!

ICHABOD. Hessian? What, you mean a German?

BALTUS. And a savage German he was, for even death itself could not hold the fury of this man, for he is ever and anon seen riding upon our roads in the gloom of night!

KATRINA. Do not frighten him, father!

BALTUS. It is for his own good that I tell him, Katrina. Are you a fearful man, Mynheer Crane?

ICHABOD. No. No. No. Just…cautious.

BALTUS. Then you had best heed what I say. Not far from here was the site of a great battle in the Revolution. Amongst the dead of this fray was a Hessian mercenary in the service of the British who was laid to rest in our churchyard. Most of him, anyway. There was one part they never found.

KATRINA. His head.

ICHABOD. His head?!

BALTUS. Yes, his head, which, with glinting blade in hand, he seeks anew each night!

ICHABOD. Have you ever seen him?

BALTUS. Oh, not I. But he has been heard several times of late, riding forth to the scene of battle in nightly quest of his head. One cannot mistake the fearsome rushing speed with which he sometimes passes along the Hollow, like a midnight blast, owing to his being in a hurry to get back to the churchyard before daybreak!

(They all turn around, and suddenly we're outside.)

(Nightfall.)

(KATRINA and **BALTUS** *stand at the door.)*

And so good night Mynheer Crane. I expect to see you at church tomorrow.

ICHABOD. Oh. Yes. Good night, Katrina.

KATRINA. Goodbye, Ichabod.

(BALTUS *slams the door.)*

(Darkness. The sound of the woods.)

ICHABOD. You see, Ichabod? It's only a story. And so, homeward.

(ICHABOD *walks. The sinister glint of predatory eyes appear behind him.* **ICHABOD** *turns. They wink out.)*

Just the candleglow from some distant windows!

(He keeps walking. A white-shrouded form flits across his peripheral vision. Then it's gone.)

A shrub...covered with snow.

(He keeps walking. The clomping of a horse behind him.)

Simply the echoes of my own feet upon the hillsides.

(ICHABOD *stops walking, but the clomping continues.)*

(A flash of lightning and the roar of wind.)

(A glimpse of the **HEADLESS HORSEMAN** *behind him.)*

Or the galloping Hessian on one of his nightly scourings?

(ICHABOD *turns, but the* **HEADLESS HORSEMAN** *is gone.)*

Merely the wind howling among the trees...

> *(The sound of snorting, hoofbeats. Lightning.)*
>
> *(The* **HEADLESS HORSEMAN** *appears again. He raises his blade!)*
>
> *(***ICHABOD** *screams.)*
>
> *(Darkness.)*
>
> *(The sound of* **ICHABOD** *'s scream is joined by an organ.)*
>
> *(***ICHABOD** *cowers on the floor of the Old Dutch Church.)*
>
> *(The* **VILLAGERS** *gather for the sermon, including* **KATRINA, BROM,** *and* **BALTUS***.)*
>
> *(Their voices form a choir.)*

VILLAGERS. Aaaaaaa – men.

> *(***PARSON VAN HOUTEN** *turns to address them.)*

PARSON VAN HOUTEN. Friends, today I was reminded how in the early hours of daylight there is a single shining star that beams when all others have muted themselves in deference to the glorious emergent rays of the sun. This star has been called Venus by some astronomers, but before receiving this pagan pseudonym the proper ancient name for this star was Lucifer. Yes, Lucifer! Bringer of light, heralding the arrival of the dawn. Once best beloved by God, this bright star deigned to shine before the sun, a pretender to the throne of heaven! Known by many names, but chief among them being the devil himself, whose sin was pride, and for which he was cast out of heaven by God. That's right. Pride! And this selfsame sin has been the undoing of many a Christian who forgets his humility and piety to God.

To succumb to the sin of pride is to allow the devil to make all manner of mischief in your life. And as the devil himself was cast out, so too will a prideful man be cast out, by his friends, his family, and his fellows, for the sin of pride is an insidious poison that no God-fearing Christian can abide. Indeed some people here may think themselves entitled to all the pleasures that the world can offer, and consider themselves superior in mind and body to all others. Such pridefulness will be their undoing, for without proper contrition they are nothing but playthings for the devil, or the devilish spirit in men, and will soon find themselves cast out from their company. Now, please join me in singing "Death Dreadful or Delightful."

(*The* **VILLAGERS** *stand and sing.* **ICHABOD***'s voice rises above the rest. Loud, triumphant, annoying.*)

ALL. *(Singing.)*
DEATH! 'TIS A MELANCHOLY DAY,
TO THOSE THAT HAVE NO GOD;
WHEN THE POOR SOUL IS FORCED AWAY,
TO SEEK HIS LAST ABODE.

(**BROM** *looks at* **ICHABOD** *and leaves the church.*)

IN VAIN TO HEAVEN HE LIFTS HIS EYES;
FOR GUILT, A HEAVY CHAIN,
STILL DRAGS HIM DOWNWARD FROM THE SKIES,
TO DARKNESS, FIRE AND PAIN!

(**ICHABOD** *holds the final note for far too long.*)

(*The service ends. The* **VILLAGERS** *mingle.*)

PARSON VAN HOUTEN. Mynheer Crane.

ICHABOD. Oh, yes, hello Parson. A very compelling service.

PARSON VAN HOUTEN. Sounds like it moved the passions of your heart.

ICHABOD. Oh, yes.

PARSON VAN HOUTEN. Sharing the word of God with those more than a half-mile off.

ICHABOD. Oh, ha ha, yes.

PARSON VAN HOUTEN. Pride, Mynheer Crane. Pride.

(**PARSON VAN HOUTEN** *exits.*)

(ICHABOD approaches KATRINA.)

ICHABOD. Katrina, may I have a word?

KATRINA. Yes.

ICHABOD. Will you walk with me?

KATRINA. Yes.

(KATRINA and ICHABOD saunter together.)

(Everyone else recedes into the distance.)

You are quite a singer, Mynheer Crane.

ICHABOD. Thank you. With a bit of training you yourself will sound as good.

KATRINA. Ah. Lovely.

ICHABOD. Pleasant day, isn't it?

KATRINA. The frosts have come. Soon all will be winter and ice.

ICHABOD. I think I saw a little snow on my walk last night.

KATRINA. But you survived.

(Beat.)

ICHABOD. Say, Katrina, ever since our lesson, I have a question I've been meaning to ask.

KATRINA. Oh. What's that?

ICHABOD. Uh, right. Well, I wonder: What…uh…well, that is to say…

(Beat.)

What can you tell me about this Headless Horseman?

KATRINA. The Headless Horseman?

ICHABOD. Do you believe it?

KATRINA. Do I believe it?

ICHABOD. Do you?

KATRINA. Do I?

ICHABOD. The Horseman?

KATRINA. The Horseman.

(Beat.)

KATRINA. *(Cont.)* The people of our valley abound with so many strange stories. It's hard to know what to believe.

ICHABOD. There are other such stories?

KATRINA. When you have been here a bit longer, you will know. To speak of such things is to court their influence in your life.

ICHABOD. But surely there must be a story or two you could tell me? If I do not hear them from you, how shall I learn them?

KATRINA. You shall discover them quite on your own, I'm sure.

ICHABOD. I suppose. Well, there was something else I had wished to ask –

> (**ICHABOD** *takes her hand and kneels.*)
>
> (**KATRINA** *suddenly steps away, distracted.*)

KATRINA. The Woman in White!

ICHABOD. Namely – what?

KATRINA. A young girl once lived very near this spot. Clever, brave, and beautiful, she was courted by many men but vowed to stay pure until she found one who would be her equal. But fate would not have it so. In the dark days of the Old War she fled into a blinding snowstorm to escape the dreadful attentions of an amorous Tory raider. In her quest for safety, she sought shelter in the ravine behind Raven Rock. The snow drifted in upon her and she went to sleep never to waken again. Ever since, her soul is said to walk along the rocks that overlook the village, in the form of a woman of palest white.

> (*A shrouded phantom passes just out of sight.*)

I can often hear her when a storm is rising, crying across the valley like the screaming of the wind.

> (*Sound of a scream in the wind. The woman is gone. Beat.*)

ICHABOD. Uh. Yes. Say, Katrina, I wonder if perhaps you would ever consider me as –

KATRINA. I must return to my father. Goodbye, Ichabod.

*(*KATRINA *exits.)*

ICHABOD. Augh! Damn. Damn. Damn me! How am I to woo the girl if she will not remain still long enough for me to ask her?

*(***BROM** *appears in the picture frame.)*

BROM. But the wind had no answer for him. So the forlorn schoolmaster returned to his schoolhouse. But when he arrived he found the place in a terrible disarray.

(The **STUDENTS** *run through, overturning the schoolhouse. Then they're gone, leaving only the mess behind.)*

*(***ICHABOD** *looks at the schoolhouse in horror and shock.)*

ICHABOD. What the –

BROM. Every desk had been overturned, and its direction reversed, such that everything which had been one way was now another. And if this weren't bad enough, the entire place had such a foul odor of brimstone that he could barely contain his stomach.

ICHABOD. Oough.

*(***BROM** *runs into the schoolhouse.)*

BROM. Mynheer Crane!

ICHABOD. Mr. Van Brunt!

BROM. Mynheer Crane! What's the trouble?

ICHABOD. Someone has broken into the schoolhouse and turned every thing topsy-turvy!

BROM. Ha ha ha.

ICHABOD. What's so funny?

BROM. Nothing. A private joke. Topsy-turvy, you say?

ICHABOD. Yes. All the chairs, the desks, everything. Do you know something of this?

BROM. Me? No. Unless – is that the smell of brimstone?

ICHABOD. Yes.

BROM. Oh, so it's happened again.

ICHABOD. Again?

BROM. They didn't tell you?

ICHABOD. Tell me what?

BROM. Nothing. Nothing. Just an old superstition.

ICHABOD. Tell me!

BROM. Back when these lands were still rough and unsettled, an old German doctor came to this valley. They say he was trained in the ancient school of Wittenberg and fled to the New World to escape a terrible debt he owed. Well, in this very spot – no no – *THIS* very spot – where our schoolhouse now stands, he built himself a home and took up all manner of strange practices. Powerful, unfathomable practices, beyond anything you or I can comprehend. I'm told he convened with bizarre creatures and familiars in this glen, until one day his creditor appeared, dressed head to toe in the darkest black. The next day his home was abandoned, and neither the doctor nor his visitor could be found. But every now and again, peculiar events surround this schoolhouse. They say it is the soul of the doctor seeking to drive away his rivals. No one ever mentioned this?

ICHABOD. No.

BROM. You should be grateful to have been treated so lightly.

ICHABOD. Has it been worse?

BROM. Much, much worse.

> *(Beat.)*

But I'm sure an educated fellow like you has nothing to fear from such country superstitions.

ICHABOD. No no no. I'm sure you're right. A prank, nothing more.

BROM. Right. Just ask yourself:

(Deadly.)

What's the worst that can happen?

*(**ICHABOD** nods thoughtfully.)*

ICHABOD. Then I shall remain.

*(**BROM** frowns.)*

And so, there's something else I wish to ask you!

BROM. What?

ICHABOD. With all this talk of spirits, you should know that I've recently encountered a being which causes more perplexity to mortal man than ghosts, goblins, and the whole race of witches put together. Namely, a woman.

BROM. A woman?

ICHABOD. Katrina Van Tassel.

BROM. Katrina Van Tassel?!

ICHABOD. Yes. And so perplexing she is! Always most welcoming when we're in company, but as soon as we have a moment's solitude, she's gone! She is beautiful and charming, and her farm is worth more than any in the valley.

BROM. What do you know of a farm?

ICHABOD. Enough that we could live there healthy and fat for a few years, until I sold it off, packed up Mrs. Katrina Crane and headed west – to newer lands and new adventures. Done forever with the uneducated, idiotic fools of this town.

BROM. I see.

ICHABOD. I knew you would. Which is why I came to you. It has come to my attention that you, sir, are something of a bravado in this land. How do I win her over?

BROM. Are you sure you wish to woo her?

ICHABOD. Of course.

BROM. Well, Mynheer Crane, we rough unmannered country men don't know much about the genteel Connecticut way of wooing.

ICHABOD. No matter! Even one with all the uncouth endearments of a bear might have better luck than I. How can you tell such a girl you love her and make her believe it?

BROM. If I knew that, Mynheer Crane, you wouldn't be asking me now.

(They nod together for a moment. Then –.)

ICHABOD. Wait, what?

BROM. Have I told you how I out-paced the Hessian?

ICHABOD. The Headless Horseman?

BROM. Late last winter, in the dead of night, far into the witching hour, I was riding past the scarred tree of Major Andre, when there approached a nameless rider mounted on a black charger. The air grew still and quiet, with only the steady beat of his hooves resounding swift behind me. And when I turned, I saw the headless spirit, bearing fast down the country road. Leaves and branches blew aside beneath his fearsome mount, and in his hands was a fearsome scythe drawn out. Swinging wide, to take my head back to his grave with him. Well, I kicked my horse to haste and off we rode. Into the darkness of the night, the trees thrashing my face, the glowing eyes of his horse close behind me.

(Rhythmic hoofbeats.)

Ba-dum-ba-dum Ba-dum-ba-dum Ba-dum-ba-dum. We rode, miles on miles, through briar and bramble, road and valley, the headless rider ever gaining closer. And then, when he was mere inches from my horse, his savage blade one swing away from my neck, I crossed the threshold of the bridge, and the wicked ghost was gone. Unable to cross the flowing waters beneath our hooves.

ICHABOD. My God.

BROM. I am perhaps the only person to have been chased by him and survived. Do you understand?

ICHABOD. Yes.

BROM. Don't ask me about Katrina Van Tassel.

> (*Beat.*)

The sun is setting. I would stay inside if I were you.

> (**BROM** *exits.*)
>
> (**ICHABOD** *gasps with fear.*)
>
> (**STUDENTS** *enter and take their seats.*)

STUDENT. In this way matters went on for some time, without producing any material effect on the relative situation of the contending powers. Ichabod failing to catch Katrina's affection while Brom Bones sullenly resorted to all manner of waggish behavior.

While Ichabod's students, upon hearing of the schoolhouse's purported hauntings, were quick to turn this to their own advantage.

> (**ICHABOD** *remains stricken by his own thoughts.*)
>
> (*The* **STUDENTS** *whisper to each other. An idea spreading.*)
>
> (*The* **STUDENTS** *read. They make a soft, groaning sound.*)

ICHABOD. Did you hear that?

STUDENT 2. No.

> (*The* **STUDENTS** *keep working. Another sound, a bit louder.*)

ICHABOD. Did you hear that?

STUDENT 3. No.

ICHABOD. Oh.

STUDENT 4. We just want to study.

> (*The* **STUDENTS** *keep working. Another sound, much louder.*)

ICHABOD. Right. Did no one hear that?!

> (**STUDENT 5** *slowly rises and turns to face* **ICHABOD.**)

STUDENT 5. I heard it. I heard it, Ichabod Crane.

(Beat.)

ICHABOD. Um, you know, just to be safe, I think we should recess class for the day.

> *(The* **STUDENTS** *make a break for it. The room empties.)*
>
> *(***ICHABOD** *tries to control his fear.)*
>
> *(***PARSON VAN HOUTEN** *enters the school.)*

PARSON VAN HOUTEN. Mynheer Crane.

ICHABOD. Aah! Oh, Parson.

PARSON VAN HOUTEN. Having troubles?

ICHABOD. No. No, no no.

PARSON VAN HOUTEN. I saw the schoolchildren run by.

ICHABOD. Oh, I...

PARSON VAN HOUTEN. Hans Van Ripper says you think your schoolhouse is haunted.

ICHABOD. Ha. Does he?

PARSON VAN HOUTEN. Do you?

ICHABOD. Yes, well, maybe.

PARSON VAN HOUTEN. And why would that be?

ICHABOD. Well, I hear there was an old German doctor who –

PARSON VAN HOUTEN. Ah, the German doctor. Ha ha.

ICHABOD. Is it true?

PARSON VAN HOUTEN. Does it matter? I have seen all manner of things in this valley, and heard many strange stories, and whether your schoolhouse is haunted or not, such stories, they tell us something, do they not?

ICHABOD. I don't see how...

PARSON VAN HOUTEN. What is faith, Mynheer Crane?

ICHABOD. Faith?

PARSON VAN HOUTEN. Yes, faith. The capacity to believe. To accept what you cannot see or know. To understand that some things are beyond the capacity of reason.

ICHABOD. Oh, faith.

PARSON VAN HOUTEN. Do you have it?

ICHABOD. Yes. Within reason.

PARSON VAN HOUTEN. Do you have faith in the people of this town?

ICHABOD. Oh, I...

PARSON VAN HOUTEN. It would seem a necessary quality for one who instructs its youth, wouldn't you say? Because you are an educated man, Mynheer Crane, you must know that to walk the path to knowledge, one may be assailed by all manner of things. Whether small-mindedness and superstition or ghosts and devils, it matters little if these things exist in the mind or in the flesh, for in either case, their impact remains quite real.

ICHABOD. I see.

PARSON VAN HOUTEN. Do you?

ICHABOD. I think so?

PARSON VAN HOUTEN. Would you admit it if you didn't?

ICHABOD. Oh, I –

PARSON VAN HOUTEN. Mynheer Crane, fear and pride are the playthings of the devil, for to succumb to either will deter you from your duty to God. What does a man of faith care if there are devils at his back or warlocks in his schoolhouse? He will persevere, as you persevere in guiding your students to wisdom, yes?

ICHABOD. I certainly try.

PARSON VAN HOUTEN. Then do not fear these ghosts. Pay them no heed. If you are meant to remain here, you will. And if not... Well, in any case, I am confident all will be for the best – here.

> (**PARSON VAN HOUTEN** *gives* **ICHABOD** *an invitation.*)

Baltus Van Tassel has asked me to invite you to his Quilting Frolic tonight. You are expected to attend this merry-making. Farewell, Ichabod.

> (**PARSON VAN HOUTEN** *exits.*)

> (**ICHABOD** *considers the invitation.*)

(He looks down the road. It looms back at him.)

ICHABOD. But what am I to do? I cannot walk that treacherous path again. Perhaps if I prevail upon the generosity of my host.

(At the house, **ICHABOD** *approaches* **HANS VAN RIPPER**.*)*

HANS. You're a miserable wretch.

ICHABOD. I'm lovelorn.

HANS. Lovelorn?

ICHABOD. Oh to be one of those knight-errants of yore.

HANS. Of mine?!

ICHABOD. Of yore!…

HANS. Oh, yore.

ICHABOD. …Who seldom had anything but giants, enchanters, fiery dragons, and such like easily-conquered adversaries to contend with before the lady gave him her hand as a matter of course. Whereas I, on the contrary, must win my way to the heart of a country coquette, beset with a labyrinth of her whims and caprices, which are forever presenting new difficulties and impediments.

HANS. Eh?

ICHABOD. Mynheer Van Tassel is having a party tonight, and I can find no means to convince the young Miss Katrina to accept me.

HANS. Katrina Van Tassel?

ICHABOD. Yes.

HANS. You wouldn't be the first.

ICHABOD. What?

HANS. You must simply find some way to excite the passions of the blood. Be bold and show the lady. Step into the room with all the force and will of a lion. When you dance, prance with the gait of a horse, when you sing, do it with the confident tones of the eagle, and when you eat, do so with the dilating powers of the anaconda.

ICHABOD. You think that will work?

HANS. Such a display is sure to please her. It should be no trouble for such a robust man as yourself to make her happy.

ICHABOD. Yes, thank you, sir. All the ghosts and goblins of this land will not deter me, but I shall march the path to triumph. But first, I'll need to borrow a horse.

HANS. A horse? One of mine?

ICHABOD. If you please.

HANS. Let's have a look.

(HANS leads ICHABOD to the stables.)

(Walking through the stalls.) Right. Yes. Here we go. No. No. No. Ah! Here, this one. Gunpowder.

(HANS brings out GUNPOWDER. A lanky, ugly, old, cantankerous horse. Just like his master.)

ICHABOD. Charming creature.

HANS. Old and broken-down as he looks, there's more of the lurking devil in him than in any young filly in the country. Up you go.

(HANS helps ICHABOD onto GUNPOWDER.)

ICHABOD. Woah – Good, boy. Good horsie.

(ICHABOD is not a skilled rider.)

Woah, uh. Hyah. Right. Ahem… Now how to turn her affections toward me?

(GUNPOWDER turns and snorts in dismay.)

Not you! Now fear not, Ichabod. You are the master of your emotions!

(ICHABOD and GUNPOWDER exit.)

(BALTUS VAN TASSEL enters with a punchbowl.)

BALTUS. Quilting!

(The farm is a lively place, filled with laughter and food. VILLAGERS gather, including OLD MEN, COUNTRY GIRLS, and SLEEPY HOLLOW BOYS.)

(The singer and fiddler take their place. A lively tune.)

BALTUS. *(Cont.)* Partners and places everyone, partners and places!

*(Everyone partners up for a country dance. **BROM** approaches **KATRINA**.)*

BROM. Katrina, may I have this dance?

*(**ICHABOD** enters the party. **KATRINA** runs up to him.)*

KATRINA. Ichabod! Dance with me!

(She grabs his hand and leads him into place.)

ICHABOD. What? Oh, I've heard of these!

*(The song begins. **ICHABOD** is an enthusiastic dancer.)*

SINGER. *(Singing.)*
IF THE DEVIL RIDES UP TO WHISK YOUR SOUL AWAY
KICK HIM IN THE PANTS AND SMACK HIM IN THE FACE
TRY A SPECIAL CHARM TO KEEP HIS TRICKS AT BAY
KICK HIM IN THE PANTS AND SMACK HIM IN THE FACE
SO LET THE FIRES ROAR AND FIDDLE KEEP THE PACE
FOR WHEN THE DEVIL COMES, WE'LL SMACK HIM IN THE FACE
HARVEST, HEARTH, AND HOME – WE CELEBRATE WITH GRACE
FOR WHEN THE DEVIL COMES, WE'LL SMACK HIM IN THE FACE
SO TURN THE DEVIL OUT, SEND HIM PACKING FROM THIS PLACE.

VILLAGERS. *(Singing.)*
KICK HIM IN THE PANTS AND SMACK HIM IN THE FACE!

(All cheer when the music ends.)

KATRINA. Again, again!

ICHABOD. Say, Katrina…

*(But **KATRINA** ducks off.)*

No matter, I shall wait till the party dies down.

BALTUS. Friends and well-wishers all! Thank you for joining our harvest-time merry making! The quilts are made, the apples plucked, the pumpkins baked, and the pig roasted. Twenty-five years ago today, on ground only a few miles hence, the men of our valley battled the fearsome Hessian soldiers for a scrap of soil called Chatterton Hill. And as you see before you, most of us prevailed! But not before many good fellows gave their lives for the cause. Tonight, we celebrate them.

(He toasts.)

Gezondheid!

VILLAGERS. Gezondheid!

BROM. And to our generous host! Gezondheid!

VILLAGERS. Gezondheid!

BALTUS. Thank you, Brom. Now let there be dancing and music, and laughter and mirth to keep away the dark spirits of winter! So when the fire dies down, we can invite them to join us again.

(Music strikes up. People talking.)

BROM. Mynheer Crane. How is the schoolhouse? Does the ghost still trouble you?

ICHABOD. I am quite done with ghosts, Mister Van Brunt. And have turned my attentions to more earthly matters. Excuse me.

(ICHABOD approaches KATRINA.)

(BROM turns to several OLD MEN.)

BROM. Mynheers. This man is not from our valley.

OLD MEN. Oh!

(The OLD MEN approach ICHABOD.)

OLD MAN 1. Young man. You are not from this valley!

ICHABOD. I am the schoolmaster.

OLD MAN 1. I could see the confusion in your eyes when Balt Van Tassel spoke. Let me tell whereof he speaks.

ICHABOD. That's really not…

OLD MAN 1. Listen. You have heard of the Hessian?

ICHABOD. The Headless Horseman?

OLD MAN 1. The same!

(The other **VILLAGERS** *enact the tale.)*

Back in the war days, the British and American line ran often through this neighborhood; making it the scene of much marauding, refugees, and all kinds of border chivalry. In those days, there was a battalion of Hessian soldiers stationed not far from here, in the town of White Plains. And I, along with a whole regiment of American troops, stood ready for a charge to overtake those few savage horsemen. In line we could see them, patrolling a fort well stocked with muskets, nine- and twelve-pounders. Fear was thick in the air when the drum and fife began, and amidst the earth-shattering roar of cavalry and cannonshot I ran, full charge up the hill, sabre clattering at my side. From the wall of their embankment, the Hessians rained down musket shot upon us. All around me my village friends and rivals fell prey to the savage German volley. But I knew I must persevere, and drew forth my small sword. A moment later, I heard very close by the crack of a gunshot and the burning smell of powder. Some nameless Hessian officer stood mere feet from me, the offending weapon still smoking from the charge. All at once, being an excellent master of defence, I raised my sword to parry the blast, and felt a sharp clang against the steel blade, around which the musket ball did absolutely whiz and glance off at the hilt, leaving me entirely unscathed.

ICHABOD. What of the Hessian?

OLD MAN 1. Hmm?

ICHABOD. The Hessian officer who fired upon you?

OLD MAN 1. Oh, he? I turned my blade upon him, but the scoundrel must have been enchanted by some ancient Teuton magic, for he narrowly escaped that fatal thrust, and ran for the safety of his great black mount. Drawing forth his own sabre he bore down upon me, preparing to lop my head from my shoulders.

HESSIAN. Kompanie Koehler! Vorwärts!

OLD MAN 1. When only a few hoofbeats away, my life was spared by an errant cannonball.

(Boom!)

And the Hessian's head was forcibly removed.

*(The **HESSIAN**'s body falls.)*

At the close of the battle his body was brought to our Old Dutch churchyard, as it was thought the most fitting home for a German soldier of the first order, and there he was interred far from his native soil.

OLD MAN 2. They say he still ties his horse there on dark autumn nights.

OLD MAN 1. What's left of him anyway.

(They laugh. The party resumes.)

OLD MAN 3. Tell him of Van Lancker!

OLD MAN 1. Ah, he doesn't care about that.

ICHABOD. About what?

OLD MAN 3. Stories of ghosts and hauntings.

ICHABOD. Tell me!

*(The other **VILLAGERS** enact the tale.)*

OLD MAN 2. Some years ago, there was a young fellow called Otto Van Lancker. A clever, helpful lad – always pitching in when there was work to be done. One night, after a long day's chores, he was walking alone on the path near Wiley's Swamp when he heard a strange whisper through the trees. The crying of a voice in the throes of deep despair. A soft piteous cry, like one long lost, hoping to go home. When Van Lancker heard this, he felt his heart break. And seeing that there was no one on the long empty road but he, he called out –

VAN LANCKER. Halloo!

OLD MAN 2. – into the swamp. Silence. Then, a moment later he saw a flicker of light, far out into the darkness. The briefest spark, and then it was gone. Perhaps the lantern of someone lost in the muck, and although Van Lancker had no flame himself to guide his way, he stepped off the road and into the grove. Within a few steps, his boots were caked with mud, and each footfall became thick and heavy. Again he heard that voice – "Hilf mir, mein Herr" – and that same faint flicker of light. So he summoned his courage, and plunged into the very heart of the swamp. Deep into the muck he went, eels and slugs doubtless circling his ankles with every step. But however far he walked, the flicker of light remained just at the edge of his gaze. Now behind a tree, then through a patch of grasses, it would flit and disappear, only to reappear some distance off. And still young Van Lancker would step through the mire, telling himself...

VAN LANCKER. Only a few steps farther and I'm sure to find it.

OLD MAN 2. Up to his hips he strode through the mud. Then to his chest. Before long the road was entirely lost, and all sense of direction escaped him, yet on he went, guided only by that ghostly light, each exhausted step driving him deeper into the swamp. Until, in the thick of the darkness, the phantom light whisked out, and a hideous laughter filled the darkness, echoing in the night. And Van Lancker found himself alone and lost, in the darkness and the mud and the silence. They say the witching light was the head of the deadly Hessian, crying to go home, forever calling to his insensate body. Or the soul of a long-dead witch, that departed her shape before the gallows could send it to hell. But all we know for sure is that this was the last anyone heard of poor Van Lancker.

(**VAN LANCKER** *disappears. Silence.*)

ICHABOD. Really?

OLD MAN 2. As true as I stand before you.

> *(The party resumes.)*

OLD MAN 3. Then how do you know the story?

OLD MAN 2. What?

OLD MAN 3. If he was never heard from again, how do you know the story?

OLD MAN 2. Bah. You think you can do better?

OLD MAN 3. Mynheer Crane, have you heard of Old Brouwer?

ICHABOD. No.

OLD MAN 3. Hey! He hasn't heard of Old Brouwer!

VILLAGERS. Old Brouwer!

> *(The other **VILLAGERS** enact the tale.)*

OLD MAN 3. Well, Old Brouwer was a most heretical disbeliever in ghosts, refuting all belief in both God and the devil. Never had he heard a story of the supernatural, but he would say:

OLD BROUWER. I will not believe without proof incontrovertible!

OLD MAN 3. As such he was known to stride with a most unnatural confidence down even the darkest path. Well, he was on his way to Tarrytown when near unto midnight Old Brouwer passed the Old Dutch Burying Ground, where the dead reside till Judgment Day. Very near this spot is a wide woody dell, within which rives a slow muddy brook. Over the deep, black part of that stream there stands a stout wooden bridge, thickly wrapped in everlasting gloom from the shade of overhanging trees. As Old Brouwer approached this bridge he saw within the dark looming shape of a rider and his horse. Now, you must understand that Old Brouwer could not see the rider so very well, all shrouded in darkness as he was. And if he saw the glinting red eye of his infernal horse, Old Brouwer was quick to dismiss it as the reflective trick of some distant lantern.

OLD BROUWER. The reflective trick of some distant lantern!

OLD MAN 3. Within moments the rider extended his hand to offer the man a place in the saddle behind him – an offer that Brouwer, as a mark of courtesy, felt obliged to accept. Well, no sooner was Old Brouwer astride the horse than he realized the rider before him had a most alarming deformity – the notable lack of a head! Some might say that's when Old Brouwer found God. But not a second passed before the headless rider spurred his horse to a violent start and down the path they raced. A breakneck speed they rode, over fallen logs and rocks they leapt, the rider driving his horse ever faster, while Brouwer held on for his very life, fearful to be dashed to death under the fearsome hooves of the midnight charger, all the while dreading whatever loathesome destination awaited the frightened heretic. They galloped hard over bush and brake until they approached the fiendish Major Andre's Tree; at which the horseman suddenly turned into a skeleton.

>   (*The* **HEADLESS HORSEMAN** *becomes a* **SKELETON**.)

Then he threw old Brouwer in Wiley's Swamp, and sprang away over the treetops with a clap of thunder!

>   (*Thunder! All cheer and laugh! The party resumes.*)

ICHABOD. Oh.

>   (**BROM** *approaches* **ICHABOD**.)

BROM. Don't tell me you're scared.

ICHABOD. What? No. I...no.

BROM. Quivering like a sheet.

KATRINA. Brom, please.

BROM. I'm done. I know what I have to do.

>   (**BROM** *parts the* **VILLAGERS** *and exits.*)
>   (*The party dies down.*)

(BALTUS thanks the departing VILLAGERS. Soon only KATRINA, ICHABOD, and the SKELETON remain.)

SKELETON. As the roar of the hearth slowly dwindled to embers, Mynheer Van Tassel's guests made their way off into the night until only one horse remained in the stalls and Ichabod found the opportunity he had been waiting for.

(The SKELETON exits.)

(KATRINA turns. ICHABOD is there.)

KATRINA. Oh, are you still here?

ICHABOD. Yes Katrina.

KATRINA. You'd better go. It's getting late. Especially for riding alone in the woods.

ICHABOD. Yes, very well, but before I go, Katrina, I have a thing, a word, a question, I've been meaning to ask you.

KATRINA. A question.

ICHABOD. Yes, I…ahem. Ahem! It has come to my attention that I have come to your attention, and so I wish to mention that it is my intention to marry you. If I may.

KATRINA. Ha ha.

(ICHABOD kneels.)

Oh. You're serious.

ICHABOD. With all my heart.

KATRINA. Right. Well, you see, Ichabod…

(KATRINA raises ICHABOD up. She touches his face, turns his head, and whispers in his ear.)

(A moment later, ICHABOD's face falls.)

ICHABOD. Oh.

(ICHABOD is motionless.)

(KATRINA opens the door. She waits for him to go.)

(ICHABOD walks to the door.)

(He stops and turns toward her. She slaps him.)

(They stare at each other.)

(They circle each other.)

(And we're outside the house.)

KATRINA. Goodbye Ichabod.

(She slams the door, leaving **ICHABOD** *alone in the night.)*

(The **SKELETON** *enters with a lantern and* **GUNPOWDER**.*)*

SKELETON. What passed at this interview none can say.

ICHABOD. Oh these women! These women!

SKELETON. But something must have gone wrong, for he sallied forth with an air quite desolate and chop-fallen –

ICHABOD. One of her coquettish tricks?

SKELETON. – went straight to the stable –

ICHABOD. Were all her affections a mere sham?

*(***ICHABOD*** takes the lantern.)*

SKELETON. – And with several hearty cuffs and kicks, uncourteously roused his steed from the comfortable quarters in which he slept. And without looking back, Ichabod Crane rode off into the night.

*(***ICHABOD*** mounts **GUNPOWDER**.)*

ICHABOD. Hyah!

*(***ICHABOD*** and **GUNPOWDER** *ride through the woods.)*

*(***VILLAGERS*** appear in the darkness. They enact the action that follows.)*

VILLAGER. The night grew darker until Ichabod again found himself beneath the fearful Major Andre's Tree.

*(***ICHABOD*** slows his horse. A groaning, creaking sound.)*

ICHABOD. Nothing. The wind. The very witching hour of night.

(Another set of hoofbeats can be heard. **ICHABOD** *turns.)*

VILLAGER. And then he saw, in the shadowy gloom of Wiley's Swamp, the towering misshapen form of a horse and rider.

(The dark-shrouded shape of a **HORSEMAN** *emerges, mounted on a midnight charger. Silence.)*

ICHABOD. Who are you?

(Utter silence.)

Who are you, I say!

(Utter silence.)

Never mind!

*(***ICHABOD** *kicks* **GUNPOWDER** *forward.)*

VILLAGER. But when that dark traveler struck a relief against the sky, there could be no mistake:

(The **HEADLESS HORSEMAN** *rears up. A flash of lightning.)*

The rider had no head!

*(***ICHABOD** *whips* **GUNPOWDER** *forward!)*

(The **HEADLESS HORSEMAN** *joins him in the chase.)*

ICHABOD. Go! Go!

(The **HORSEMAN** *surges forward.)*

*(***ICHABOD** *drops his lantern. It crashes in the distance.)*

(Suddenly, **GUNPOWDER** *turns sharply.)*

VILLAGER. With a sharp turn, Gunpowder plunged into Wiley's Swamp.

ICHABOD. Aaah! No no no!

VILLAGER. Along the sandy riverbank they rode.

(A jarring ride. The **HEADLESS HORSEMAN** *gives chase.)*

(ICHABOD crashes through low-hanging branches.)

VILLAGER. *(Cont.)* Just then Ichabod saw a break in the trees beyond:

ICHABOD. The churchyard! If I can but reach that bridge, I am safe!

> *(The HEADLESS HORSEMAN raises his blade as he draws near.)*

VILLAGER. And with a final convulsive kick, old Gunpowder sprang upon the bridge, leaving behind the fiendish Horseman – unable to cross the flowing stream below.

> *(GUNPOWDER clomps onto the bridge. Sound of the stream below.)*
>
> *(The HEADLESS HORSEMAN looms in the distance.)*
>
> *(ICHABOD turns around. Out of breath, but triumphant. He looks at the HEADLESS HORSEMAN.)*
>
> *(GUNPOWDER struggles free and runs off.)*
>
> *(ICHABOD starts to laugh. Relieved, triumphant, haughty.)*

The Horseman reared his mighty steed and sent his frightful head aloft!

> *(The HEADLESS HORSEMAN throws his head. A ball of orange flame. ICHABOD screams in horror as the hellish light consumes him.)*
>
> *(Darkness.)*
>
> *(The sound of the stream.)*
>
> *(As the misty morning light creeps up, ICHABOD is gone.)*
>
> *(The VILLAGERS gather. They watch the river.)*

VILLAGER 1. Old Gunpowder was found without his saddle, and with the bridle under his feet, soberly cropping the grass at his master's gate.

VILLAGER 2. But Ichabod did not make his appearance at breakfast.

VILLAGER 3. Dinner-hour came, but no Ichabod.

PARSON VAN HOUTEN. The children assembled at the schoolhouse, but no schoolmaster.

VILLAGER 4. Hans Van Ripper began to feel some uneasiness about the fate of poor Ichabod.

HANS. And my saddle.

VILLAGER 1. An inquiry was sent on foot, and after diligent investigation they came upon:

HANS. A saddle trampled in the dirt.

BROM. The tracks of horses' hoofs deeply dented in the road.

KATRINA. The hat of the unfortunate Ichabod.

BALTUS. And a shattered pumpkin.

> (**BROM** *laughs darkly.*)
>
> (*The* **VILLAGERS** *look at him.*)

BROM. I'm sorry. It's funny.

VILLAGER 2. The brook was searched.

BROM. But the body of the schoolmaster was never recovered.

HANS. Hans Van Ripper, as executor of his estate, examined the bundle that contained all his worldly effects. They consisted of:

VILLAGER 5. Two shirts and a half.

BROM. Two stocks for the neck.

VILLAGER 4. A pair or two of worsted stockings.

VILLAGER 3. An old pair of corduroy smallclothes.

VILLAGER 2. A rusty razor.

PARSON VAN HOUTEN. A book of psalm tunes.

KATRINA. A broken pitch pipe.

BALTUS. And Cotton Mather's *History of Witchcraft* in which was a sheet of foolscap much scribbled and blotted in an attempt to compose verses honoring Katrina Van Tassel.

HANS. All of which were forthwith consigned to the flames.

(A roar of flame.)

VILLAGER 1. The school was removed to a different quarter of the Hollow, and another pedagogue employed in his stead.

BALTUS. And except for this, life in the valley resumed without change.

KATRINA. Well, one change:

*(**BROM** takes **KATRINA**'s hand and goes to one knee.)*

BROM. Katrina, will you marry me?

KATRINA. Yes, Brom. I think I will now.

(All cheer!)

PARSON VAN HOUTEN. But what happened to Ichabod Crane?

VILLAGER 1. Many surmise that he had been carried off by the galloping Hessian.

VILLAGER 2. Recall the stories of Brouwer, of Bones, Van Lancker, and others.

VILLAGER 3. And as he was unmarried and carried no debts, most people afterward thought little of it.

BROM. There was an old farmer who came back from New York to report that Ichabod Crane was still alive – that he had left the neighborhood, changed his quarters to a distant part of the country, studied law, had been admitted to the bar, turned politician, electioneered, written for the newspapers, and finally had been made a justice of the Ten Pound Court.

VILLAGERS. Ah.

HANS. I can see that.

KATRINA. But! – the old country wives, who are the best judges of these matters, maintain to this day that Ichabod Crane was spirited away by supernatural means, and the ghost of the unfortunate pedagogue still paces his decaying schoolhouse. They say, on a still summer evening one can still hear his voice at a distance, chanting a melancholy psalm among the tranquil solitudes of Sleepy Hollow.

(The stream burbles.)

(KATRINA *sings the hymn. Beautifully.)*

(Singing.)

DEATH! 'TIS A MELANCHOLY DAY,
TO THOSE THAT HAVE NO GOD.

(KATRINA *conducts the other* **VILLAGERS**.*)*

VILLAGERS. *(Singing.)*

WHEN THE POOR SOUL IS FORCED AWAY,
TO SEEK HIS LAST ABODE.

(ICHABOD *is heard whistling the tune. Distant, shadowy. His footsteps echo in the old wooden schoolhouse.)*

(The **VILLAGERS** *listen in fear.)*

(KATRINA *turns and smiles.)*

End of Play

Death! 'Tis a Melancholy Day

Music: Tim Cameron

If the Devil Rides Up

Music: Tim Cameron

♩=120

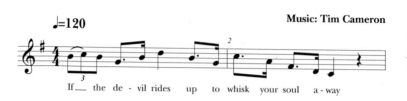

If— the de - vil rides up to whisk your soul a - way

Kick him in the pants and— smack him in the face

Here's a spe - cial charm— to keep his tricks at bay

Kick him in the pants and— smack him in the face

So— let the fires— roar and fid - dle keep the pace For

when the de - vil comes,— we'll smack him in the face

Samuel French

Har - vest, hearth, and home___ we ce - le-brate with grace___ For

when the de - vil comes___ we'll smack him in the face

So turn the de - vil out, send him pack - ing from this place

Kick him in the pants and___ smack him in the face.